THE FIG THIEF

A Book of Poems

GUERNICA WORLD EDITIONS 92

THE FIG THIEF

A Book of Poems

GABRIELLA M. BELFIGLIO

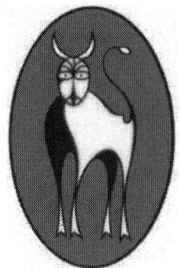

GUERNICA WORLD EDITIONS
TORONTO • CHICAGO • BUFFALO • LANCASTER (U.K.)
2025

Copyright © 2025, Gabriella M. Belfiglio & Guernica Editions Inc.
All rights reserved. The use of any part of this publication,
reproduced, transmitted in any form or by any means, electronic,
mechanical, photocopying, recording or otherwise stored
in a retrieval system, without the prior consent of the publisher
is an infringement of copyright law.

Guernica Editions Founder: Antonio D'Alfonso

Michael Mirolla, editor
Cover design: Allen Jomoc, Jr. | Cover art: Julia Weekes
Interior design: Marg Suarez, www.margsuarez.info

Guernica Editions Inc.
1241 Marble Rock Rd., Gananoque (ON), Canada K7G 2V4
2250 Military Road, Tonawanda, N.Y. 14150-6000 U.S.A.
www.guernicaeditions.com

Distributors:
Independent Publishers Group (IPG)
600 North Pulaski Road, Chicago IL 60624
University of Toronto Press Distribution (UTP)
5201 Dufferin Street, Toronto (ON), Canada M3H 5T8

First edition.
Printed in Canada.

Legal Deposit—Third Quarter
Library of Congress Catalog Card Number: 2025932036
Library and Archives Canada Cataloguing in Publication
Title: The fig thief : a book of poems / Gabriella M. Belfiglio.
Names: Belfiglio, Gabriella M., author.
Series: Guernica world editions (Series) ; 92.
Description: First edition.
Series statement: Guernica world editions ; 92
Identifiers: Canadiana 20250153149 | ISBN 9781771839655 (softcover)
Subjects: LCGFT: Poetry.
Classification: LCC PS3602.E42 F54 2025 | DDC 811/.6—dc23

Dedicated to Priscilla (Petrullo) Belfiglio, my mom,
who read to me my first poems,
opening a portal into worlds of words.

"I'm the woman
with Monday-night bags
hanging off her wrists.
I smell like figs."

—Ladan Osman

Contents

I

Riding the Staten Island Ferry 3

II

Thread 7

Cut Short 9

My Anthonys 11

Orphan Train 12

My Internal Ancestors Forbid: 13

Buona Pasqua 14

Fragile 15

Down the Shore 16

How Many Eggs Did You Use 17

One Good Meal 18

B35 to Brownsville 20

Up Against the Wall 21

III

Prodigal Lover 25

The House Guest 27

Erasure 29

Descent 31

My Father's Father 32

Matin 35

Acherontia Atropos 36

Before the Dove 37

Why Are There So Many Poems About Birds 39

Arms Like Amelia 40

La Bailarina 41

The Light of the Moon 43

Run Your Hands Through This 44

Liberation 46

The Peach Tree 47

The Fig Thief 49

When We Were Still a Family 51

V

Sex Life of Figs 55

VI

Husband and Wifey 59

Wide Open 60

This City Is My Lover 61

Cruising Christopher Street 62

Good At Biting 63

Before Winter Comes 64

Doing Laundry Together 66

Seismic..67

Dumped 68

Basin 69

Exposed 70

The Near and Far 71

Positive...72

Places to Land 73

Instructions After Death 75

Begin Again 78

VII

Grace...81

~ • ~

Notes...85

Acknowledgements..86

About the Author 91

I

"atlas of bone, fields of muscle,
one breast a fig tree, the other a nightingale
both morning and evening"

—Natalie Diaz

Riding the Staten Island Ferry

I shift as close
to the bow
of the colossal ship
as they allow.
Over the orange rail, I dip
my body, imagine arriving
a century ago,
like my kin. How, with only
a suitcase memory of home
they were cast to begin again.
Ash of Etna
in the crevasses
of their worn-leather shoes.
A new terrain bestowing
the copper lady of the East River,
Goddess of wayfarers,
who caravans abroad the weary.
Her right arm
ever resists gravity
her torch sings
through tempests
waving the promise
of sated bellies and gold springs.
I pray for deliverance
above the sea.
Against my face,
the wind feels like flying.
My lover's worried,
grabs hold of my shin.
She would stride to
cage me, never leave
my side. Be the air
I breathe. My arms
              rise in full swing. It's too late,

      I'm free

II

"A strangler fig
Do homeless ancestors
live inside the tree?"

—Hoa Nguyen

Thread

My *nonno*, Antonio, was a tailor; I don't know
    who taught him, or where he learned to sew,
not even sure on which hemmed shore.
    At sixteen, he crossed the Atlantic
leaving behind his parents and seven
    siblings in a town so small it barely
has a name. Randazzo — the same
    as an old Italian restaurant
in Sheepshead Bay. I have a half-used
    book of their matches on my nightstand
as a reminder to go there
    as if it will unlock some mystery.
I hesitate, afraid of no connection
    to my ancestors' Randazzo.
I'd rather live in the what if.
    I wonder the crazy what ifs my *nonno*
pondered on his way to America,
    in the lowest deck of the San Guglielmo.
He arrived on February 9th, 1912,
    was seasick the whole journey over.
For Christmas, I acquire a print of his boat
    and after my mother carefully refolds
the red and green paper, for next year,
    and figures out what she is holding,
she starts to cry — which, in turn, draws drops
    from my own eyes to the chagrin
of the rest of our family.
    As an adult, I learned to copy their reserve,
so unlike my years as a child
    and tears would storm my face,
back when my *nonno* was my protector;
    I remember the pillow of his belly
and the feeling like nothing bad could happen.
    He died on Christmas Eve, I was twelve.

I dreamed his dying and when my mother came
        into my room to tell me, I thought
I was still dreaming. That was the same year
        I lost my sister, but here I am lacing
multiple sorrows, a web I keep weaving
        where I am spider and fly at once,
when I was trying to reveal
        my *nonno's* adept hands and his sewing
machine with a foot pedal I loved
        to practice pushing. He made clothes
in a corner of South Philadelphia,
        sent his profit home to a corner
of Sicily, a corner as precise
        as a fitted shirt, tailored just right.

Cut Short

> "To name oneself is the first act of both the poet and the revolutionary. When we take away the right to an individual name, we symbolically take away the right to be an individual. Immigration officials did this to refugees; husbands routinely do it to wives."
>
> —Erica Jong

Listen to the names:
Antonio,
  Vincenzo,
    Luigi,
      Maria,
        Giovanni,
          Giuseppe,
            Carmella.
Taste them inside your own mouth, it's glorious.

They were children when they left.
Antonio first, 16,
with only a sharp needle,
giant ball of red thread, and
steady grip.

As Antonio swayed over the waves
he slowly wove together bits of string,
weeds, anything he could find—
until the rope thrown
to his family
was strong enough
long enough
to reach the other side of the world.

They climbed over—
rough calluses like islands hardened
across the soft of their palms.
Antonio's fists
never letting go, grew

red and sore, as he
anchored them ashore.

In American schools
during a time dagos
were not yet considered white.
Teachers coined names that were easier to say—
Lou, Joe, John, Jim (from Vincenzo—
the one I could not understand).

Flat. Like a slap
across the face.

My Anthonys

1195
Patron saint of children,
poor people,
prisoners,
glass blowers,
people who've lost something,
and barren women.

1896
A boy of 16, leaving one island
for another. His mother pushes him
from the blood of WWI,
into the blood of a coarser war: America.
He exhausts days on streets of South Philly,
sews other people's clothes, mails money
home, a lifeboat for his family.

1940
Too short a childhood—so many siblings
behind him, the job as father:
a tight skin forced to stretch on.
His own at 20—surprise!
Then another and another and another,
Until his wife's tubes are tied. Thirty years
grading math tests, running marathons,
dreaming of living in the woods,
falling asleep at the kitchen table
red ink staining his elbow creases.

1971
The boy. Three sisters.
And like air, music.
Always music.
A gift.
Hours spent
his fingers breathing
the keys of the piano.

Orphan Train

When someone claims
I don't look like my parents,
my father eagerly explains

where they found me.
I picture a small child
playing with prairie grass

by railroad tracks
She's holding a blanket or doll;
maybe it's a tattered

bear. Sometimes she misses
the chug of the train.
Pines for the chorus

of her cohorts crying. Yearns
for a hand to clutch.
My father likes to engineer fictions.

A compelling story can pin
my attention more than anything.
He delivers the punch

line with a grin
that slides into his chartreuse eyes:
stranded at the last stop!

Sometimes the child is oblivious.
Absorbed with the singular motion
of pulling, her fingers

like a vise
on either side
of thin blades.

My Internal Ancestors Forbid:

1. Allowing a stranger to mispronounce your name, without correcting them

2. Using jarred spaghetti sauce

3. Choosing the pack of pomegranate seeds someone else plucked from the goddess' fruit

4. Throwing away the plastic bag your bread (or anything else) comes in when you can rinse it out and use it again

5. Buying packaged pre-washed greens

6. Trashing your ripped stained t-shirt when it will make a perfect rag

7. Drying clothes in a machine on a sunny day

8. Discarding used wrapping paper instead of carefully slitting the scotch-taped seams and folding it into a functional pile next to the saved ribbons, boxes, …

9. Paying someone to clean your house

10. Refusing food someone you love offers, even if you just ate and hate peas, you spoon into your replete mouth the entire mound, until your plate is bare

11. Denying the magic of September light after families call children to dinner and there's a patch of ivied fence slanting a rectangle of sun

Buona Pasqua

After an

afternoon of clean laundry

that smells like the sun and antique

shops, images of my nanna and nonno float

near me. I see them smiling as we pile out of the

car and swing open the silver gate. In the yard the

sheets blow on the line —banners of childhood. I dash to

deliver hugs and kisses. On the Porch there's iced tea and

shiny aluminum cups waiting — I search mine out from

the middle of the pyramid — pink. My nanna squeezes

a lemon into the glass. The smell of dinner sneaks

through the screen door and I start to tingle

— gleam as bright as my new

white shoes.

Fragile

I kick off my shoes,
drag the red, cat-scratched chair,
climb atop, reach the fancy teacups
displayed on the tallest shelf of the bookcase.
Take down one decorated with trailing klameria,
nanna's favorite. She chose
it from the eclectic collection
kept in her corner china cabinet.
I always selected the scalloped cup
with leafy vines that traveled in and out
of porcelain valleys and hills.
We only ever used them after church.

At the big family dinners,
she staged a matching cerulean and white set.
She would hardly recognize me now —
with a scattering of gray hair,
cut to the scalp, and a middle-aged ring
around my once tiny waist.

Who will drink from this cup
after I'm gone? Who will secure
the delicate handle and as gently as a surgeon,
fit the curved bottom back to its devoted saucer
after taking a sip?
For this cup will surely outlive me
as it has *nanna*
and the person she bought it from
and the person who shaped it
and the one who painted by hand
the perfect burgundy flowers.

Down the Shore

The unruly ocean extends past our pocket
of New Jersey, beyond sight.
It disappears into a blurry line
of blue, sea and sky overlapping.

The older cousins fan out a threadbare
sheet, strewn with stitched bouquets.
They slick their skin with baby oil,
arrange their bodies in flat strips;

glittery bikinis wink at the sun.
My brother and I part
to find Styrofoam soda cups
in the dented metal trash cans

by the crowded boardwalk.
We gather as many as we can carry,
dash back through hot sand,
build castles on water's salty edge.

At the rented house,
a block below the painted merry-go-round horse,
our *nanna* is making it ours.
On the stove simmers

a robust pot of tomato sauce;
in the palms of her hands, meatballs roll.
Neatly gathered, two white braids
stretch across her head.

How Many Eggs Did You Use

I am making *gnocchi*,
my grandmother's *contadina* hands
are embodying my own.

I scoop out thick
ricotta, taste
the white mess.

Later, I smother
the tiny dumplings in red
carry them to my guests.

They raise forks
to lenient lips.
Before plates are cleared

I offer a second heap,
hear my grandmother's
affect: *What, you don't like it?*

One Good Meal

Past live chickens in crates on 148th Street
children romp at Martin Luther King Playground.
Dream of swings becoming doves
they   will   fly.

Stray cats shelter beneath jungle gym bars
after the children dash toward
the smell of charred cheese
steering them home.

A dishwasher from the corner bodega
plunks a pile of leftover rice
in front of cat's paws,
they nudge in their whiskered faces.

In a diner with neon lights —
one the shape of a fork —
people eat next to
pictures of Ali and Ross.

The waitress asks
"you want a warmup honey?"
her hair in a bun under a net.
She's already tilting the pot.

There's a line for the crowded Bx19.
An apple escapes as the wheels
of a shopping cart struggle up steps.
A passenger searches for quarters

to pay the fare. The woman
with her mini restaurant on wheels,
parked in front of the check-cashing
awning, reaches into her trolley,

and like Mary Poppins,
pulls out an array of items in a flash.
Hot sauce squirts perfectly onto
her customer's steaming enchilada.

B35 to Brownsville

I love my country.
The United States.
I don't complain.
I don't complain about my lifestyle.
The United States,
this is my country.
Fifty-three years in this country.
I'm going to Flatbush.
Flatbush Avenue.
I don't carry a lot of money.
Just what I need.
Just what I need for my food,
my clothes.
I have it.
I keep it in the bank.
I have it,
I just don't carry a lot.
Just what I need.
I am Fifty-three years old.
I'm getting old.
I'm nearly dead.
Dead Man Walking.
You gonna live it,
you gonna die it.
You spend your money.
I spend my money.
FLATBUSH!
Flatbush Avenue.
Getting off.
Getting off by Citibank,
Yes, this is *my* neighborhood.
I hang out over here.
I hang out over here all the time.
Right here.

Up Against the Wall

Men line up as early as 7am
on Church and McDonald
by the looming Astoria Bank
or the seedy bar across the street.
Some hold paper cups

filled with deli coffee:
something to keep fingers warm.
Others stuff hands into pockets
of hoodies, as they shuffle their feet.
Beat-up boots kick stale butts off the curb.

They skirt the flood of children
lugging backpacks almost as large
as themselves, yanked by
mothers that tug winter coats
over saris or sweatpants.

The laborers relocate their bodies
to dodge the rush of business suits
and shiny thermoses that push
to the subway, overhear
private conversations shouted

past cell phones.
To pass the time they talk about
fútbol; José is rooting for Mexico.
Victor bets on Brazil—his smallest boy
is sure they'll win.

Every time a van slows they
shoot up, eager to be chosen,
eyes more hopeful than
that kid in gym class,
desperate not to be left for last, again.

By 10am after vans
have come and gone
those left slump against the wall,
baseball hats cushioning the feeling
of something hard against skull.

III

"I wanted to crawl in between those black lines of print, the way you crawl through a fence, and go to sleep under that beautiful big green fig-tree."

—Sylvia Plath

Prodigal Lover

I wake to untamed rain
flooding my head.
I love the music
of the drops

on the aluminum awning
canopying this house
where we met.
I listen in bed for hours.

The downpour turns
the curb's edge into a river
like the kind
my brother and I

raced sticks down
sprinting to the end
of the block
to see whose won.

I wonder why
you're streaming
into my life again

as it's starting
to burst forth,
if I want you to.

Different gender,
no cocaine,
same electricity
when I'm near you.

For my birthday
you bring *Interpreter of Maladies*,
soft chocolate-chip cookies,
slow R&B,

show me the stitches
that criss-cross your chest
like a treasure map.
You ask if
I want truth or lies,
I say both, knowing
that's what you're best at.

The House Guest

Here's the scene:
I'm at my girlfriend's sister's house,
it is Memorial Day—
the American flag
flaps red, white, and blue
like a warning
at the front door.

The backyard is full of glee—
children splashing pool water
into the hot Florida air
like fountains. Their parents
mingling: margaritas cold
in the cup of their hands.

I'm sitting on the back porch
trying to remember
not to call my girlfriend
honey or *sweetie*. I don't
dare sit next to her,
even though everyone knows.
I am not the first girl
she's brought home.

Her sister introduces me
to the neighbors
as *the house guest.*
I find a baby to hold, hide inside
rocking him to sleep. The weight
is satisfying—his balmy skin
sticks to my own. Long after
his eyes have stopped fluttering,
I cradle the half-moon body.
I am doing ok until
my girlfriend's mother
passes me a camera.

She finds me, in a crowd,
hands it to me.
It is a calculated move.

*Will you take a family picture
for us?* she asks smoothly.
My girlfriend gathers amidst her
parents, her sister and brother-in-law,
the two little ones in front.

A stranger approaches,
Here, she says reaching
for the camera,
*don't you want to be
in the picture?*
I will the tears that surge
into my eyes to stop,
crouch on the other side
of the pool—close to
the water's edge,
aim and shoot.

Erasure

I.   We are forbidden to bring in lighters, matches, scissors, razors, knives, personal medications, glass bottles, glue, knitting needles, rug hooks or embroidery, firearms, liquor, marijuana or drugs, fingernail polish or remover, aerosol cans, lighter fluid, or cameras.

The guard behind the front desk warns me to be careful—pointing to my belly seven months full of growing baby.

II.   Lisa is happy to see us, for once. As usual, she immediately asks if we brought cigarettes. When she hugs me, I feel bone.

III.   Cell by cell, I've been watching her die for more than two-thirds of my life. Longer than I've lived in Brooklyn. Longer than I've lived any place, or than the tree that towers beyond my apartment has been growing, or than people have been dancing to *Thriller*, or viewing *The Simpsons*, or Bono's been singing about streets with no names, or Madonna preaching to women about deserving the best in life, or we have been watching Thelma and Louise triumphantly drive off their cliff, or Spike Lee telling us to do the right thing, or witnessing William Hurt kiss Raul Julia in *Kiss of the Spider Woman* or Whoopi Goldberg kiss Margaret Avery in *The Color Purple*, or Natalie Goldberg's been advising us to bare our bones, or we have been tasting Anne Carson's bittersweet, or been lost in Toni Morrison's middle passage, or solving the six sides of the Rubik's cube, and much longer than we've been using cell phones, iPods, YouTube, blogging, Facebook, and email. I have been observing my sister die longer than Lady Gaga has been alive or Georgia O'Keeffe has been dead.

IV.   We meet in the hospital lounge. My father, next to my mother, then Lisa, her caseworker, and a social worker, around a square table. My girlfriend and I sit on two cushioned chairs along the wall close by. A team of four young interns in official white coats and nametags stand on the other side of the table.

As they discuss business, Lisa drags her chair in between Margarita and me. Lisa tells me she's going gray in the same place I am. She tears her chair over to our mother's side, interrupts the conversation. She has something *really* important to tell her. And just as fast spins back to me and asks if I will buy her a Diet Coke from the machine downstairs. She can't sit still; still, it is the longest I've seen her so contained in years. She tells me she cannot wait to get out of this place—that it's been months and they all drive her crazy. She looks hesitantly over to Margarita and tells her it's nice to meet her, not remembering when, about a year ago, she viciously pushed her out of the room.

Lisa leans closer to me and asks if I know who the father is. She tells me I can call her any time if I need to talk. Afterwards she scrapes her chair to our father's side, climbs onto his lap as if trying to erase 40 years. His body turns to stone.

V.   How many times have I tried to write this poem?

VI.   Before we leave, Lisa releases the chain from her neck, a gift from her *boyfriend*. She says she's sorry it got a little messed up from the shower—loops it around my neck, the rusted silver heart dangles into the hollow of my clavicle.

Descent

"Get Inside
Before I Fucking
Knock You Out,"
my middle-aged neighbor
screams at her granddaughter.
The little one is wearing
a purple dress that falls
in line with her knees' creases.
Yellow polka dots
on the collar
frame her neck.

A shrill wail escapes
as she sneaks away.
She crouches behind
the decaying Chevy.
"Don't Start That Shit Now—
You're Gonna Get It
Even Worse
If You Don't Shut Up."

Later the girl
grinds her crimson sandals
into the pavement
steadily killing
a colony of ants
who are constructing hills
between cracks
in broken concrete.

My Father's Father

> "To even write father
> is to carve a portion of the day
> out of a bomb-bright page."
>
> —Ocean Vuong

I don't know what to call you,
despite the fact you are my kin.
Grandpop I suppose, though, I never got to

meet you. I've tried to learn more details, but very few
have stories, at least not ones they easily throw in.
I don't even know what to call you.

I know you were wounded in World War II,
and that you often drank tall glasses of gin.
Grandpop, I never got to

look in your eyes and see their unique hue,
or hear you play your mandolin.
I don't even know what to call you,

with only my imagination as proof.
I've heard you frequently knocked your youngest son askew.
I suppose, I never even got to

hear your side. But I cringe at the rumors where you screw
up the loving family that somehow always made do.
I don't even know what to call you.
Grandpop, I suppose, though I never got to.

IV

"What sweeter world could be voyaged from
the earth's center, pieced of figsuckle,
orange, the twice-licked skin of key limes,
breath of peppermint, braided, burning."

—Nikky Finney

Matin

Early morning belongs
to the clouds. Left over
mashed potatoes warming
on the stove. A fried egg
shimmers into solid white—
its yolk measles
a giant yellow eye peeking—
like through a windowpane
to galloping wings
outside. Sparrows
music back and forth
tree to railing
in the shape of a rainbow.
The sun yawns awake
cracks through.

Acherontia Atropos

--African Death's-Head Pupation

At the moment of transformation,
how do we release
skin the color of sunshine?

Or trust that without
these sticky legs—we could
possibly move forward?

Isn't it easier to grasp
what we know?
To revel in the shadow

of our admirer's eyes?
Easier still to inch our way
back to the familiar

branch—bark comfortable
and solid beneath us?
It takes more than wings to fly.

Before the Dove

I was the first herald launched.
This is my tale.

After the sedulous rain
quieted to a drizzle,
I rose from swaying ark,
terrified of returning empty-
beaked. I felt need
of land purl through every plank
of our boat. The giraffes
were tired of jamming their supernal
necks against the low ceilings,
no leaves to chew.
The lions' claws used to
meeting blood and bone,
lay uneasy and dull inside
supple paws.

And Noah.   Noah ached with
the desire of covenant. Standing
on the highest mast, his eyes
quivered with each wave
erect on the salty horizon.
In bed next to his wife,
Noah dreamt of dirt.
Each rising of the sun
a persistent murmur bid   patience.

I flew over lustrous waves —
bluegreen ripples shaped like
wings. Searching, I flew.
The air ghostly still.
Water stretched endlessly,
in all directions.
The current raised giant claws
to capture me.

I soared above, merging into night sky,
dark as my own Raven feathers.
I flew into its giant swallow,
as if there were a place to land.

Why Are There So Many Poems About Birds

Because we all want
the skills of Superheroes—
Do we envy the science

of a wing span—
Or the avian magic
of abandoning gravity—

Is it that words fail us—
And only a high-pitched trill
through air can thrill—

Do we crave a nest
of tangled twig—
A concave mattress of moss—

Always a tree manifest—
Maybe we aspire to bare
our cumulus breast to the wind

shadow the coast
of a brackish marsh—
Or, seize a muddy worm

from a garden bed
to feed our young
from our own barbed mouth—

Or because—
Hope is the thing
With feathers--

Arms Like Amelia

                                         stretch back

                 reach—   arms become

                  wings   catch the air

              draw the breath   out of

              those two pillars   shoot like an arrow

                 extend   wide

               span decades   she swooped above

      the Atlantic, stunning   the skeptics that tried

           to hold her down   swish

         13 hours 30 minutes   I knew I had to fly

La Bailarina

I.
Swirling in front
of San Juan market
a shower of limbs,
gold dust, iron rods—
tangled on wet street.

Aureate
fluttering of wings,
from deep inside
a silver streaked
butterfly escapes.

II.
Pain,
blood,
doctors,
operations,
casts.

White straps wrap
across breasts,
silver buckles press
into skin,
plaster corsets—
restrict everything:

*I had to learn
to keep still.
I watched death
circle my bed.*

III.
Wand, magic in her
hand—movement
returns as paint.
Stick figures, lines thin

like her broken spine.
In the background
of paintings
a strip of blue sea
a buoyant promise.

The Light of the Moon

for Audre Lorde

Imagining your lips—
my mouth words oaths
that loosen like the leaves of autumn
dry   falling   and full of color

I have always been a spring person—
yellowgreen—more day than night
skin not as bold as olives
nor as light as peaches

I have mourned the end of summer
like a lover gone—preparing
my limbs to be covered in cold neglect,
the impending dark a hole akin to a grave

But in your Earth an ancient spirit rises
your words come like rain
and I find myself drenched
sink my toes deep into rich reds and browns

In the growing twilight
I move forward a little taller
less with the anticipation of joy
more a warrior's stride of determination.

Run Your Hands Through This

> You only have to look at the Medusa straight on
> to see her. And she's not deadly. She's beautiful
> and she's laughing.
>
> —Hélène Cixous

this   head

              of   snakes

                                       come closer

                  they don't   bite

          this
     twist

          this
     frizz

                     this rope men climb

       this
   mask

                                       camouflage

crown of fem in in it y

                        these   wild   ringlets

curled   wands   that   charm

          doors
                open

                        the same ones that without these locks
          lock in my face

this net
              web

                        pile

it's getting   heavy

Liberation

It's time to start over.
New names, hilarious and sharp.
We have to pursue growth.
    How much?
Maneuver off the cliff.

       With fists as well as
       Hands.

Let the waxing crescent
of light
       disclosed by the stars and the silence
guide us impossibly far.

We have seen plenty of fights.
       There are so many roots to the tree of anger.

Take to the road. A truly
visceral experience awaits.

We are emerging
right before your eyes.
Look again.

No longer can you
bridge our backs for gain.

       We endure, this we are certain of.

We're balancing at the precipice.
Calling on Eos to launch us
exactly where we need to be.

The Peach Tree

It started with a pit
from *La Festa Della Madonna Nera*
at Phoenix Bar in the East Village.
We sing, laugh and lay out offerings
in a make-shift altar
bid for the dark goddess.

Annie brings peaches
from her grandmother's tree in Yonkers.
She orders: *Have one—enjoy—*
but you got to promise to plant those pits!
I save mine in a cocktail napkin,
like the number of a hot girl:

pert ripples leave
an indelible impression
on white. A year later,
on my Brooklyn balcony,
I am potting tomato plants.
I spot a wispy shoot.

I tug it out.
Hidden in the dirt: the pit.
It's split in two.
There is an offspring growing:
nothing less than a miracle.
I replant it. It expands every day,

till the tree is taller than the railing.
Her leaves, bright as fire, fall into fall.
Her empty branches point
toward her Bronx backyard,
toward a corner of Sicily
where the Madonna rests,

or maybe toward any earth below,
where she can freely expand her roots.

Just before the first frost,
she rides to Philadelphia.
I present her to my father.
He plants her in his mini orchard

that you see as you drive
the sweeping stretch
to my parents' house.
A house that I've never lived in.
Framed in the upstairs bedroom
is a picture of the ship

my *nonno* sailed in from Sicily.
In processions with weary voices
praying for miracles,
on impossibly narrow streets
he followed many madonnas,
envisioning third legs they must be hiding

under their billowing black skirts.
The last time I saw the tree
she was still small,
but it won't be long
before she becomes
an unmistakable welcome,

here,
she'll say,
you're almost there,
rest a moment.
Tempt:
have a peach.

The Fig Thief

My father and I tread concrete
squares home from the store
milk heavy in his hand—

I've just moved here, brought
everything that could fit
into his car—boxes from Hasan's

bodega, *Corona, Budweiser*
crossed out, and my name in black
marker, followed by a list:

Books: Poetry: Brooks to Dove;
Wintry clothes: Nonno's brown sweater,
long underwear.

The last boxes crammed
with the scribble of: *MISC. ITEMS.*
I bring warm wear anticipating

the season changing, not knowing
if another transport will happen
before then—now it is muggy:

We are in shorts.
I am the one who picks
the only ripe fig—the branch

is leaning over the sidewalk
as if we were meant to find this tree—
the two of us—still, I think back

to that time I was a child
walking home from elementary school
lost in song, collecting flowers from front yards

to surprise my mother.
When I turned down my street
with the pink house at the corner

my bouquet was plump and bright.
Before I could see her smile
my father's homily blast—

HowcouldyouWhatisWrongwithyou?
I had no idea what I did wrong
just that I did.

I take a bite of the soft fig
the crunch of seeds in my teeth—
yield the remainder to my father.

When We Were Still a Family

1.
We are smiling, My brother and I
in matching red and cream outfits.
Clothes sewn by our *nanna*
from the same bolt. My sisters wear
fashions of the 70s. Everything in mini.
Shoulders and thighs exposed.
Eight opaque eyes focus straight ahead.

2.
We shared a house, ran up
and down the same stairwell. Every night,
ate dinner around the breakfast-room table.
I sat between my father and Lisa.
Under the table, my brother
kicking me messages.
No one dared complain or laugh,
breaking the silence.

3.
There's a naked wall behind us.
No backdrop of blue skies and sun
or Cinderella's castle.
None of us had any idea
of what the world would demand.

4.
It's over two decades since all four of us
have been in the same room.

5.
I still lace my fingers the same way:
one talking to the other
speaking in a dialect the rest of me
must translate.

6.
Loretta wraps her arm round the side
of Anthony's waist—claims him.
On the other side,
I'm caught between Lisa's knees.

Her hand holding me is
cropped out of the picture.

V

"Her breasts bloom
figs burst
sun is white
I'll never come back"

— Lawrence Ferlinghetti

Sex Life of Figs

1.
I track fig trees   map of desire

branches weighted with ripe   figs
arch above backyard fence
too high to reach

          silent sirens

how not to bruise   delicate skins
    full-grown figs too fragile to travel far

plucked fig, egg sac, alive,
          still warm from sun
laden with sweetness

cameo pink seeds
as surprising as lips
      of vagina

in broken   open   heart
of the inky   fruit

a thousand female flowers
fill my mouth

2.
Even Moses' mother must have
chewed and swallowed
this plump fruit

figs   among oldest of joys to be bit into,
     gritty nectar skimming tongue

nature's sugar carried
to the new world by monks
spread by the poor

as sinless as Eve

3.
Aristotle's tiny female wasps
    beckoned by the fig's aroma
    struggle inside
to pollinate,

the XX external internal
blossoms,

sacrifice their lives

    girl on girl

4.
my wife constructs a tool
from a broken broom handle
and plastic water bottle,
    sphere scissored out,
to cleverly capture
what is out of reach

    I fall in love again

VI

"Empty your basket of figs. Spill your wine."

—Ellen Bass

Husband and Wifey

Shmoogedy Shmoggedy
Gertrude and Alice B.
kept house with modesty
in Paris, France.

Never claimed (either one)
bisexuality.
Alice wore flowered hats,
neither wore pants.

Wide Open

Have you looked close?
Your losses will cloud your judgment.
Once you reach newfound options
you should ask the woman behind them
etched in anger and sorrow,
to dive into unexplored territory.
If you're afraid, you are encouraged
to sit and draw. Perhaps read
something insanely beautiful, rising
against the evening sky.
An ocean of darkness.
Once you harbor it in your body,
overflow space—
steal the show.

This City Is My Lover

I walk on her streets and let her curves carry me. The red and green of streetlights direct me, I move in and out of crowds almost invisibly. Down 3rd Avenue suits and highheels are getting off work. They push to the steps of the subway; I leave them underground where coats are stained a scummy gray-black. The setting sun shines gold into the windows. It is magic. Something good inside buildings that clack with the sound of beating keys and drown with deep monotone voices discussing your and my life as if they knew how it felt. Fluorescent lights blare and coffee is carried to them by that *hot new secretary* with long blond hair, *did you notice the way her ass moves when she walks?* I chop my mane short, shake my limbs rid of the ooze of filth that tries to stick to my skin. I walk in shadows past corners of people sleeping in boxes, living off unfinished lunches left in Styrofoam containers thrown away in front of their faces. I sit on the benches in the park on East 16th Street, watch methadone addicts get their latest fix. This city is full of mistakes just waiting to happen again. Sometimes it hurts to keep your eyes open. I walk her chaotic streets and the power encompasses me. I whisper to her in earnest,

Beloved.

Cruising Christopher Street

I ride the subway to find you. Beneath the city, your station: grimy walls frame ceramic confetti, mosaiced into bohemians and rebels. Above ground, men in leather and feathers blaze windows. Shops flash big hair, big heels, big dicks. Rainbow flags curtain the glass panes of bars. *The Village Cigars* store wraps around your corner—where one could buy pastel cigarettes, the kind my ex-girlfriend sported in college, hoping no one would bum a turquoise smoke. Dear Christopher Street, folk musicians siren your name. Those weary rest in Sheridan Square, shaped like a triangle. Instead of soldiers riding horses clenching chin-raised poses, your statues are intimate: two men and two women holding hands. After dark your pulse rises—blood flowing from Greenwich Avenue to the Hudson. A perpetual beat: past into present and present ever new.

Good At Biting

She liked to play good girl/
bad girl. She didn't like poetry,
all that swallowing.
I would be tipsy outside my brain.
Scattered one-night stands
in the bathroom stall, three
in the back of my closet,
several that get mislaid
in the rush.
Like a dream
where my cheeks blush
redder than her red convertible.
Ring around a four-poster bed
to a parallel universe, a thrust of white
clouds a blanched landscape.
Send me fleshy emails—
refill my wine glass till the bottle
burns into the body.

Dress me up in shades of sin.
Drive too fast—
jump start my heart—
thunder my throttle.

Before Winter Comes

We ride the subway up the alphabet
to the edge of Brooklyn. She tells me
life and death stories. The pastel shirt
she's wearing is soft between my fingers.
I picture her dropping a daisy
on her father's grave, veer my body
across the orange seats into her.

Jellyfish are strewn along the shoreline,
hiding amongst the discarded round
bottoms of glass bottles. If you look
closely, you can see a ring of electric blue,
thinner than a spider web, encircling
their gelatinous bodies. I am shocked
with childhood fears, as my bare feet tiptoe

through the squishy landmines. Behind us,
the Cyclone towers above signs hawking
cold beer and hotdogs, above the crooked
brown of the boardwalk, above her and me
tangled into each other, our bodies
pressing down the faded leopard-skin-
patterned sheet, into the supple sand.

A tribe of Hasidic children in matching shirts
and skirts, invades our otherwise naked
beach. The girls scatter away from their mother
and the baby she is holding to search
for shells and other treasures. Three boys
play catch, each throw bringing them closer
to our embrace, pretend not to look.

In the morning, I am salty
from her kisses. The ocean and sand
switched places overnight
land became liquid
dripping into my shower drain
and the sea
a scratchy solid on my skin.

Doing Laundry Together

The day I leave for school, we go to the 24-hour laundromat—the big one on Washington. I leave her to sorting, go in search of coffee. At Tom's Diner people are grouped in twos and fours, a colony of squawking seagulls gulping pancakes and eggs, not as lucky as the others who flew out of the city for the long weekend. It is the end of summer, and the very air is different not just in temperature and light, but in people's breath—a collective sigh clouds over the neighborhood. I could walk these streets blindfolded. Every corner has a reminder, like a flashcard, of somebody I have loved or hated or both. I return with the coffee, just the way she likes it—black one sugar. The clothes are turning in the wash. When we woke up I lingered longer in bed than usual; I moved my body close to hers. I could navigate her landscape blindfolded. But she insisted there were dirty clothes I would need mixed with hers and we left the apartment laden with heavy bags.

Seismic

I am on the verge of ruin.
Lava hardened around
wildflowers, treeroots, and travelers

like poured concrete.
Fire, dormant inside.
Days land like rapid punches.

an upwelling. A deadness—
ash and air—try to resist gravity.
Warm up, get ready

to launch. I have learned
to survive in dark places.
Me, little stone pieces of Etna

molting into myself.
I want the igneous earth to shift,
send me swirling.

Dumped

I find a hole to live in,
on 18th Street in Brooklyn.
To pay for the dump, I get a job.
I walk around the hours of the day—
a magic trick—cups and balls.
My roommates, a colony of cockroaches,
just out of grad school,
have been watching me for weeks.
I shred or file hulking stacks of papers.
I collect smooth stones
outside the journalism building.
Mostly I wish to steal
one night of sleep from the dead
in clothes that don't fit me.
I deny the truth as long as possible.
I am suspended by the sun,
severed from you.

Basin

I tell myself: become a gypsy
wear billowy skirts, string bells
around ankles, weave hair
with deep-colored ribbons—
plum crimson charcoal.

Carry little:
pack a knife
and don't leave
without books
full and empty
of words.

Follow the Mediterranean Sea—
the shape of your pelvis.
Cover your skin with the scent
of jasmine and keep walking

even if feels like a maze
even if it feels like
you will never escape
moving in circles
round and round
the same shitty path.

Find a ripe
lemon or fig
and let it become
your mouth.

Maybe if you don't expect to feel
at home at the end of the day
it will hurt less.

Maybe you won't feel alone
if you look into every set of eyes
like a friend's.

Exposed

beyond the abandoned ball fields

there is the familiar breath

I free my lungs

join the trees

pitch deeper into leafcrunch

spartan limbs unmask sky

one points toward me

or is it past

I ask: *who else*

did you witness today

last year

prior century

she keeps pointing

The Near and Far

after Tu Fu

Unseen cicadas ululate
into the late-August wind
which blows toward
Ocean Parkway
its fast flow
of cars lap
back and forth
back and forth
between shores
their waves crash ferociously
or threaten to from afar
only to fizzle
into a soft white foam
when no one is looking
or when they are
it makes no difference
to the sea who sees
who's never known
what time the clock reads
yet across time
keeps on keeping it
mixing rain
and tears
and salt
and sweat
and tires
that sing a song
you can only hear
if you're submerged
if you admit
that that boundary
between you and me
she and he
solid and liquid
doesn't really exist
sing along

Positive

When you feel it you know
something is terribly right
dire luminosity
You might be nauseous—
your stomach
somersaulting for gold
Settle into a frantic calmness
Time the jump of your heart
beat the pace it takes
to run the subway stairs—
first out the turnstile
The trouble comes with thinking
Remain brilliantly ignorant
With your outstretched arm
shape the vernal air

Places to Land

The morning sun beams
a slanted rectangle of light
on our cream-colored wall.
It looks like an entryway.

The pre-teen on the F train
wears black polka dot tights.
The crossing and uncrossing of her legs
orchestrate the words from her lips.
She frees a kiss on her friend's cheek
before she scoots off the orange seat—
her backpack barely clearing the closing doors.

The lady in a business suit
coos *good girl* to her tiny dog
as a taxi buzzes past
the corner of 16th and 5th—
her hand, covered
in a blue NYT plastic bag, at the ready
for her dog's concrete-scratching
ritual to end.

Union square is still calm—
only the peal of metal poles
as they puzzle together.
A man in a fluorescent green vest
whistles into the straggling crowd,
directing the wheatgrass van into its spot.

A Goldilocks fillet of flounder—
not too big, not too little—
perches on the scale
as the farmer's market customer,
wearing her everyday pearls, beckons:
pack it inna bit of ice. A fishmonger
scoops some into the open bag.

A gaggle of preschoolers press
toward the front of the case of fish,
hoping to see something
they have never seen before.
Eww! they chime—eyes greedy
for a glimpse of guts.

A black-olive ring falls
from the corner of its pita
onto the gravel. An eager squirrel
scuttles close—ready to retrieve.

A rush of people maneuver
stand to stand—piling into bags
the ingredients for tonight's dinner.
A loose onion rolls
under a tower of collard greens.

Crowded subway home,
a honey-headed woman sits
with her legs draped
across her boyfriend's lap.
They take up more room than two people.
Thumping bass leaks from
his earphones. She twists closer
as a lady thumps onto the seat
on her opposite side.

I arrive back
to three hungry cats and the smell of garlic.
I kick off my boots, dump my backpack
on a chair, and undress, collapse
into a tub full of steaming water.

My sweetheart dishes out white rice.
She sneaks a pink shrimp into her pink lips
before sliding the rest on top.
Our tiger-striped cat, lounging
on the kitchen table, jumps off
just in time for the plates to land.

Instructions After Death

1. Save one part of the firewood of my body—
   You choose:
   clavicle, nipple, elbow, clitoris, heart.

2. Offer the remainder to science—
   what's functioning, give away,
   answer someone's prayer.
   If it's too late, bring my cadaver
   to a hospital with eager students,
   let me be touched one more time,
   eyes curious to see what's inside.

   Let them cut open, beyond skin,
   and like a poem in a foreign language,
   read each recognizable vein, follow
   the skinny slippery route up my thick thigh
   down my solid spine,
   make a sliver of sense of our mysterious body.

3. Burn the part you saved.
   Have song in the background,
   like at a campfire—Joni Mitchell or Nina Simone.
   If my brother is alive, rent a grand piano.

4. Separate the ashes into three.

   Carry a third to Italy,
   measure out a teaspoon
   of the dried basil of my body.
   Sprinkle it into the Arno river,
   under that massive weeping willow
   there on the edge of Florence.

   Head south.
   Keep me in your pocket.
   Walk the streets,
   look up and down instead of left and right.

Notice the art under your feet,
colors above your head.

Talk to people along the way,
use your eyes, your hands,
the tilt of your head,
don't use English.
As you walk away, say:
sta mi bene,
your fingers still reaching.

When you find Mt. Etna growing
out of the tiny village of Randazzo, shed me.
There will be ash here already, mix mine in
with bare hands—like how you make meatballs.
Give it a little spit in place of egg to make it stick.

5. Return to America.

   Retrieve the second third.

   If it's winter, head to the Brooklyn Bridge.
   Here you must have a plan.

   It is not as easy as you think to fling
   contents into the East River.
   There are cars zooming below you,
   a web of metal enclosing you—throw strong
   with a full arc of motion.

   If it's summer, take the F train to Coney Island.
   Buy something awful, like cotton candy
   or a Nathan's hot dog, or battered
   fried shrimp with more batter than shrimp.
   Maybe go on a ride or two. (I would do this first, however.)
   Sit in the sun, and when you are ready
   run past the mass of people, through the shallow waves,
   till you can dive into the Atlantic Ocean whole—
   empty me here.

6. With the final dust of my ashes,
    go to Philadelphia, where I started.
    Find Giovanni's Room, sit by the window,
    read someone remarkable
    like Audre Lorde or Adrienne Rich.
    If you find my book, recite
    something from here too.
    Afterwards, find a private area of Fairmont Park.
    And with a seed of a fig tree,
    bury me.

Begin Again

Snowflakes bigger than
Susan B. Anthony silver dollars
plummet with torrid speed.
On this spring day, I let
go—submit myself
to something bountiful
something the snow is listening to
and allow the thoughts that come to haunt
fall and melt as they hit the sidewalk.
Right now I am standing in the
cold feeling fat drops
on hair that tickles my forehead,
I close my eyes aware only
of light and wet
and infinite possibility.

VII

"... Past the city and out into the orchards
Where perfect figs and plums ripen
Without fear..."

—Tracy K. Smith

Grace

Around the table,
home-made wine is poured and passed.
Children whine with delicious need.
In a singular moment of silence,
my aunt asks if anyone wants to say grace.
I think of my cousin
whose bulging left calf
displays a burly inked cross,
or my godmother
who has a tiny gold
one circling her pink neck,
or my wife who was forced to church
each Sunday of her childhood,
or my brother who has found God
as an adult and reads
his Bible every day like practicing
the stretch of octaves on his piano.
Surprising myself, I immediately offer.
I thank my Aunt Marie, hosting us —
all in two parallel tables crammed into her cozy dining room —
I thank everyone present,
for being so, I thank the farmers for the food,
and I stop after I quickly extol
the universe itself.

I don't mention God.
My grandmother, sitting a few folding chairs to my left,
who's approaching one hundred, softly comments:
I always thanked the farmers too
remembering a different decade.
I'm overcome with love for her and this gravid family she's created.
Some of us have died.
Some have been in prison.
Some have fought in wars.
Some of us have protested war in front of the White House.
Some of us have physically attacked others at the table.
Some have physically attacked themselves.

Some of us have PhDs and some never finished high school.
Some of us have not been able to stay out of rehab.
Some sneak cigarettes and convince themselves no one will notice
their smoky breath when they kiss goodbye.
Some have just started talking.
Some have said things they regret.
Some of us judge some of us without ever saying a word.
All of us have forgiven someone here for something
we have now forgotten.
With a chorus of *salute,*
glasses click into a crescendo of chaos.

"We hid among tangerine peels, lamb bones and blue figs."

—Carolyn Forché

Notes

"Cut Short": Epigraph quote from How to Save Your Own Life by Erica Jong

"My Father's Father": Epigraph quote from "Deto(nation)" by Ocean Vuong

"Run Your Hands Through This": Epigraph quote from "The Laugh of the Medusa" by Hélène Cixous

"La Bailarina": Italicized text from The Diary of Frida Kahlo, compiled and introduced by Carlos Fuentes

"Liberation": Italicized text (in order) from:
    "Women" by Alice Walker.
    "Poem About My Rights" by June Jordan
    "Who Said it was Simple" by Audre Lorde
    "narrow path into the back country" by Diane Di Prima

Acknowledgements

Much gratitude goes out to editors, journals, anthologies and publishers who have published these poems or their earlier versions:

"Cut Short," "Before the Dove": *Gravida*

"Down the Shore," "Boundaries": *Challenger International*

"Grace": *Palabras Luminosas* (ANYDSWPE Anthology Series)

"Erasure": W.B. Yeats Contest Poetry Contest Winner (guest judge Jessica Greenbaum) and *Headcase: LGBTQ Writers & Artists on Mental Health and Wellness* (Oxford Press)

"The Fig Tree": *Foglio* (AU)

"Cruising Christopher Street": *Hashtag Queer Anthology* (Qommunity LLC)

"The Near and Far": *Comstock Review* Special Merit Poem

"Before Winter Comes": *Chiron Review*

"Husband and Wifey": *The Careless Embrace of the Boneshaker* (Great Weather for Media)

"Places to Land": *Roanoke Review*

"Matin," "Acherontia Atropos": *Folio (BPL)*

"Wide Open": *E•Ratio*

"La Bailarina," "My Father's Father": *Italian Americana*

"The Light of the Moon": *Radius*

"Seismic": *Thick With Conviction*

"Hope": *Nomad's Choir*

"Instructions After Death": *Poetic Voices Without Boundaries* (Gival Press)

"Descent": *Ghost Fishing: An Eco-Justice Poetry Anthology* (University of Georgia Press)

"Exposed": *Iodine Poetry Journal*

This book has been a long time in the making. I am eternally grateful to all the brilliant people who have helped me along the way, whether with inspiration, feedback, multiple drafts, nuts and bolts, and/or support and love: this book has finally come to fruition because of you.

I thank Michael Mirolla and the Guernica publishing family for selecting, believing in, and creating a home for my book.

I thank Allen Jomoc Jr. for his cover design.

I thank my community from Antioch College, where I started to bloom as a writer.

I thank my peers and teachers from American University MFA program. Especially Myra Sklarew and Keith Leonard.

I thank my peers and facilitators in the various Brooklyn Public Library workshops I have attended. And the Library itself—a true refuge.

I thank MALIA: this radical network of talented Italian and Italian-American women artists and scholars has been a vital source of knowledge and inspiration.

I thank the Brooklyn Society of Ethical Culture Writers Group, especially Kim D. Brandon, who has been a steady force and source of encouragement and inspiration.

I thank the Literary Outlaws for Liberation (LOL) group of writers for all the insight and solidarity. (Secret handshake forever!)

I thank my 100-worders! It is always a joy to read your voices and have you witness mine, especially Mitch del Monico, who has kept the torch lit and takes the time to connect.

I thank Maria Lisella and all from the Italian American Writers Association (IAWA) for bringing valuable voices forward and for always making me feel welcome and valued as a feature.

I thank Emily Sernaker for her insight and joy while studying poets new and beloved to me.

I thank Greg Newton and Donnie Jochum for fostering queer books and the people that love them: The Bureau of General Services—Queer Division (BGSQD) has been a safety net in this sometimes scary world.

I thank Drae Cambell for their essential queer storytelling event, Tell, and for giving me a space to tell my stories.

I thank JP Howard and the Women Writers in Bloom Poetry Salon for their embodiment of grace and power.

I thank Rachel Zucker and the 92nd Street Y class she fearlessly led. And those from that group who have become a bedrock of my writing life— my "Green Room Group," especially Marion Brown, Deb Hauser, Olga Rukovets, Marc Tretin, and Jocelyn Casey-Whiteman.

I thank my *meravigliose* Ferlinghetti Girls (Phyllis Capello and Paola J. Corso), for their wisdom, creativity, collaboration, and friendship.

I thank Brooklyn Poets and the perceptive Eugenia Leigh for helping me turn my manuscript inside out and find a content and order that was hiding inside.

Bonnie, thank you for your mutual love of words and life stories, and for our endless conversations.

Beverly, I am thankful our friendship has survived past high school and continues to thrive. I thank you and Haskel for your boundless solidarity.

I thank the inimitable Annie Rachele Lanzillotto— whose continual encouragement, love, and wisdom keeps me going.

I thank the wondrous Julia Weekes—who not only provided the beautiful cover art but also has been my soul sister, there for me in ways I didn't even know I needed.

I thank my chosen family—the celebration of and freedom to be true to ourselves is essential in this world that is always trying to coerce you into a box to check off.

I thank my large extended family and ancestors who have helped shape who I am.

Anthony, thank you for all the music.

Carol, Aunt Marie, Loretta, Dad, your companionship and support over the years has been indispensable.

I can't imagine my life without my immediate family: Marg, Emmett Agostino, and Kali Antonia. You have each made me into a stronger and fuller person. The love I have for you each is more expansive than words.

My work has been informed, inspired, and molded by so many amazing writers who I haven't mentioned yet. I am lucky to have found you and your creative geniuses. To name just a few:

> K. Addonizio / E. Alexander / M. Alexander / E. Bass / E. Bishop
> G. Brooks / E. Cardwell / A. Carson / P. Cavalli / T. Chang
> V. Chang / C. Clarke / T. Derricotte / N. Diaz / E. Dickinson
> S. Dolin / R. Dove / N. Finney / M. Flaherty / C. Forché
> T. F. Ford / S. Gilbert / M. M. Gillan / N. Giovanni / E. Giunta
> L. Glück / J. Graham / M. Hacker / N. Handal / J. Harjo
> Y. Harvey / J.C. Herman / J. Hirshfield / M. Howe / J. Jordan
> B. Kingsolver / J. Lahiri / J. Larkin / D. Laux / A. Limón
> L. LoLo / A. Lorde / D. Maraini / E. S. V. Millay / D. Minkowitz
> G. Mistral / M. Moore / T. Morrison / G. Naylor / N. S. Nye
> S. Olds / G. Paley / L. Pastan / M. B. Pratt / A. Rich
> M. Rukeyser / M. Sarton / W. Shire / P. Smith / T. K. Smith
> W. Szymborska / G. Timpanelli / A. Walker / J. Winterson / V. Woolf

— oh, and so many more.

Thank you cats of the world who have saved me when words could not.

And finally, I thank you, reader! Without you, this pursuit would exist in a hollow place. Thank you for taking time with these words — for giving them a place to land and expand beyond the page.

About the Author

Gabriella M. Belfiglio is an Italian-American queer artist, poet, and activist.

Her work explores moving into lesbian self-hood, finding home in untraditional places, and deep playful language, often with a narrative delivery. Her writings call attention to the multifaceted nature of identity.

Gabriella's poem "Erasure," earned her a Yeats Poetry Prize awarded by the WB Yeats Society of NY.

She was awarded a Saltonstall residency fellowship in Ithaca, NY, and she received Special Merit Recognition in the *Comstock Review's* Muriel Craft Bailey Poetry Contest.

Her manuscript, *The Fig Thief,* was a finalist for the Luria Frasca Prize (Bordighera Press) and 3 Mile Harbor Press Prize.

Her poetry and creative non-fiction have been published in numerous anthologies and journals including: *The Centrifugal Eye, Potomac Review, Poetic Voices without Borders, Lambda Literary Review, The Paterson Review, Mutha, Avanti Popolo, Folio, Grande Dame, Typehouse, Gravida, Cacti Fur, Mediterranean Poetry, The Shanghai Literary Review, The Stray Branch, The Roanoke Review, Grabbing the Apple, Slant, Pinyon Review, Chiron Review, Literary Mama, Monterey Poetry Review, Italian Americana,* and *One Breath Rising.*

Gabriella has been the featured reader at The Cornelia Street Café, Bluestockings Bookstore, The Nuyorican Poets Cafe, The 92nd Street Y, Barnes and Noble, Queer Memoir, *Tell* at BGSQD, Brooklyn Society for Ethical Culture, IAWA, Lesbian Herstory Archives, 440 Gallery, Judson Memorial Church, Brooklyn Lyceum, Parkside Lounge, and Fresh Fruit Festival, among other venues.

Gabriella is a founding member of the Sicilian-American activist/poet trio, The Ferlinghetti Girls, with Paola Corso and Phyllis Capello. Together they have performed at Soapbox Gallery, Principles GI Coffee House, The New York City Poetry Festival on Governors Island,

Washington Square Park, Coney Island Boardwalk, guerilla outdoor settings, *cantastoria* tradition—bringing poetry alive and making it accessible to the everyday person.

Gabriella trained at Brooklyn Women's Martial Arts and The Center for Anti-Violence Education in Goju Karate and self-defense. She is a seasoned instructor who has practiced and studied conflict resolution and de-escalation extensively through her work as a teacher. She has been rooted in social change working with populations who experience violence most: underserved communities, queer homeless youth, survivors of domestic violence, mentally challenged individuals, and more. Her fierce warrior vision is to make the world a better place for all.

Additionally, she teaches ethics, literature, creative writing, and art. Her non-traditional work brings Gabriella to all corners of the five boroughs of NYC and beyond.

Gabriella was born in Philadelphia, PA. She is the youngest of four siblings. She attended Antioch College, completing a BA in poetry and gender studies. While there she worked at the acclaimed *Antioch Review*. She earned her MFA, in poetry, at American University.

She lives in the Sunset Park neighborhood of Brooklyn, NY, overlooking the beautiful Green-Wood Cemetery. She makes a home with her nontraditional family, including their clowder of feral cats.

Web: www.gabriellabelfiglio.info
Instagram: @gmbelfiglio